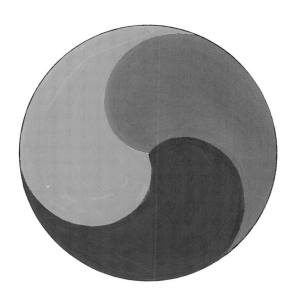

THE
KOREAN
CINDERELLA

by Shirley Climo
Illustrated by Ruth Heller

HarperCollins*Publishers*

For Sarah SuYun Manthey—
the real Korean Cinderella
—S.C.

To Helen and Don Reid
—R.H.

I am indebted
to the International Cultural Society of Korea
and particularly to Keum Jin Yoon,
for her impeccable organization of my itinerary,
and to Woon Sook Cho, who is also known as Daisy.
—R.H.

Library of Congress Cataloging-in-Publication Data
Climo, Shirley.
 The Korean Cinderella / by Shirley Climo ; illustrated by Ruth
Heller.
  p. cm.
 Summary: In this version of Cinderella set in ancient Korea, Pear
Blossom, a stepchild, eventually comes to be chosen by the magistrate
to be his wife.
 ISBN 0-06-020432-X. — ISBN 0-06-020433-8 (lib. bdg.)
 ISBN 0-06-443397-8 (pbk.)
 [1. Fairy tales. 2. Folklore—Korea.] I. Heller, Ruth, date, ill.
II. Title.
PZ8.C56Ko 1993   91-23268
398.2—dc20   CIP
[E]   AC

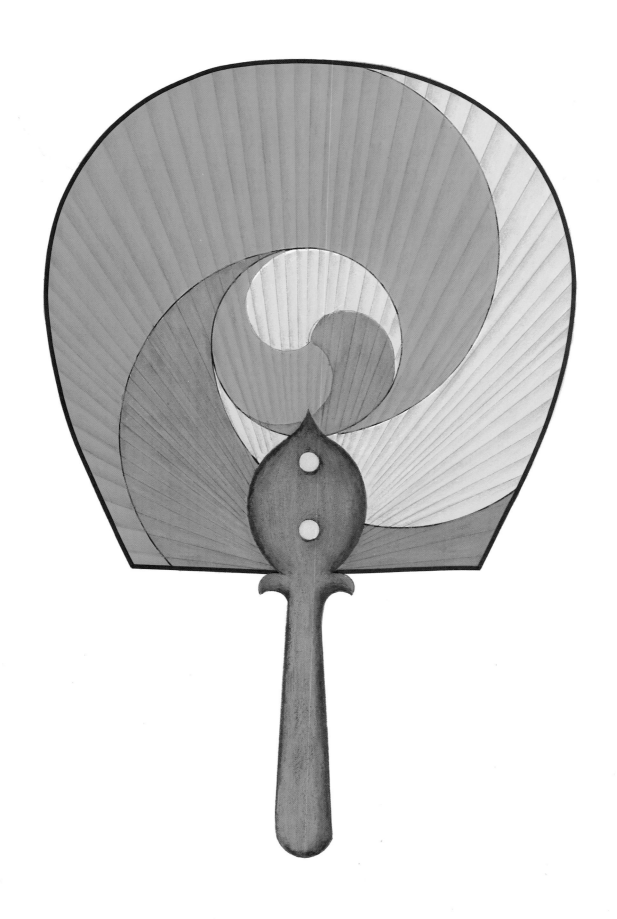

LONG AGO IN KOREA, when magical creatures were as common as cabbages, there lived an old gentleman and his wife. For years they longed for a child to share their tile-roofed cottage. At last a daughter was born.

"Good fortune!" the old man exclaimed. "I'll plant a pear tree in the courtyard to celebrate this day!"

"And Pear Blossom will be our daughter's name," the old woman added.

Both the tree and the child grew lovelier with each passing season. In spring white flowers frosted the tree, and Pear Blossom wore a white ribbon on her long, black braid. In summer, when the tree bent with ripening fruit, Pear Blossom's mother wove a band of rosy gold into her hair. In the autumn, when leaves from the tree blew about the courtyard like scraps of sunshine, her mother dressed Pear Blossom in a yellow gown. But one winter day, when the branches on the pear tree were still bare sticks, the old woman died.

"*Aigo!*" wailed the old man. "Who will tend Pear Blossom now?"

He put on his tall horsehair hat and went to the village matchmaker. She knew of a widow with a daughter. The girl, named Peony, was just the age of Pear Blossom.

"Three in one!" promised the matchmaker. "A wife for you and a mother and a sister for Pear Blossom."

So the old gentleman took the widow for his wife. Although Pear Blossom called the woman *Omoni*, or Mother, she was far from motherly. And Peony was worse than no sister at all.

Omoni found fault as soon as she stepped into the kitchen. "Too cold!" she grumbled. "The fire's gone out. Fetch wood, Pear Blossom. Be quick!"

Pear Blossom gathered sticks and fed the stove until the lid on the kettle danced from steam.

"Too hot!" her stepmother scolded then. "The noodles are scorching. Get water, Pear Blossom. Be quick!"

Both Omoni and Peony were jealous of Pear Blossom, and the harder she worked the happier they were. Each day Pear Blossom was up before *Hai*, the sun. She cooked and cleaned until midnight, with only the crickets for company.

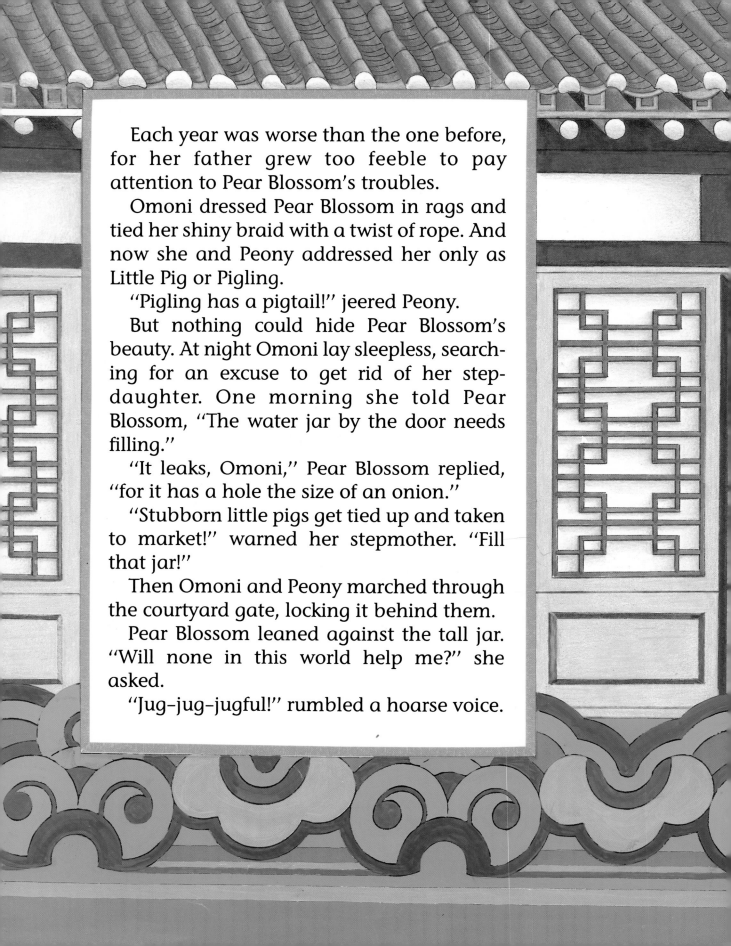

Each year was worse than the one before, for her father grew too feeble to pay attention to Pear Blossom's troubles.

Omoni dressed Pear Blossom in rags and tied her shiny braid with a twist of rope. And now she and Peony addressed her only as Little Pig or Pigling.

"Pigling has a pigtail!" jeered Peony.

But nothing could hide Pear Blossom's beauty. At night Omoni lay sleepless, searching for an excuse to get rid of her stepdaughter. One morning she told Pear Blossom, "The water jar by the door needs filling."

"It leaks, Omoni," Pear Blossom replied, "for it has a hole the size of an onion."

"Stubborn little pigs get tied up and taken to market!" warned her stepmother. "Fill that jar!"

Then Omoni and Peony marched through the courtyard gate, locking it behind them.

Pear Blossom leaned against the tall jar. "Will none in this world help me?" she asked.

"Jug-jug-jugful!" rumbled a hoarse voice.

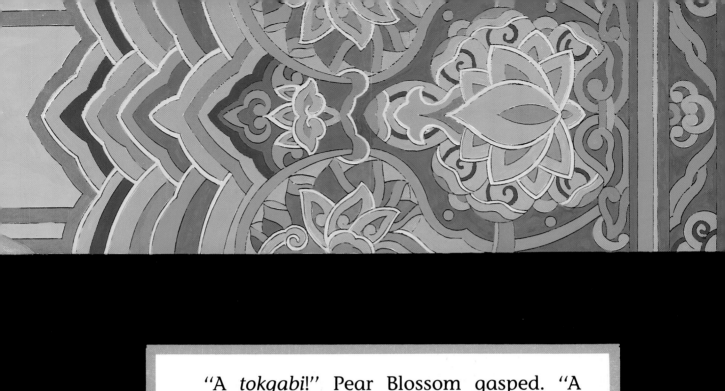

"A *tokgabi*!" Pear Blossom gasped. "A goblin!" What if a tokgabi goblin were hiding in the jar? Fearfully, she stood on tiptoe and peered inside.

A gigantic frog with bulging eyes stared back. "Jugful!" it croaked again, and squeezed itself like a stopper into the hole in the jar.

"As you wish," agreed Pear Blossom, for, frog or goblin, it was best to do its bidding. She hurried to the well and drew a jugful of water. When she poured it into the jar, not a drop leaked out!

When Omoni and Peony returned, they found Pear Blossom resting beside the jar. "So!" Omoni shrilled. "Off to market, Little Pig!"

"But Omoni, the jar is full," Pear Blossom protested. "A frog helped me."

"Trickery!" snapped her stepmother, but she muttered to Peony, "A magic frog! Look inside that jar!"

Peony hung over the rim but saw only her own scowling face. All of a sudden the jar tipped. A flood of water soaked Peony from head to toes. "Pigling's to blame!" she howled.

"Someday Little Pig will get what she deserves!" Omoni declared. She made Pear Blossom crawl through the puddles, licking up the water.

The next morning Omoni scattered a huge sack of rice around the courtyard. "Hull this rice, Little Pig," she ordered. "Polish every grain. Or else"—she shook the empty bag—"YOU'LL be put in this sack and sent to China!"

Then Omoni and Peony left for the village.

Rice covered the ground like sand beside the sea. Pear Blossom threw her arms around the pear tree and asked, "Will none in this world help me?"

Wings whirred overhead, and a flock of sparrows flew out of the tree. "Cheer! Cheer! Cheer!" the sparrows called to Pear Blossom. They pecked at the rice, separating husk from kernel. In a matter of minutes the sparrows had polished the rice and piled it in a corner.

When Omoni came back, she found Pear Blossom nodding beneath the tree. "Off to China!" her stepmother began, and then caught sight of the mound of rice. "How can this be?" she demanded.

Pear Blossom rubbed her eyes. "Sparrows flew out of the tree and polished the rice."

"Birds don't hull rice," scoffed Omoni. "They *eat* it!" But to Peony she whispered, "It's magic that's flying about! Catch some!" She pushed Peony beneath the pear tree.

At once the cloud of sparrows swooped down. "Cheat! Cheat! Cheat!" they chattered at Peony. They pecked at her, tearing her jacket. They perched on her head, pulling her hair.

"Pigling's to blame!" Peony bawled.

"Someday Little Pig will get what she deserves!" Omoni threatened. She did not give Pear Blossom anything to eat, not that day or the next, not so much as a kernel of rice.

Pear Blossom had food to fix nevertheless. The village was having a festival, and she had to pack picnic hampers of dried fish and pickled cabbage for her stepmother. She also sewed a dress of pink silk for her stepsister. When festival day came, Peony mocked Pear Blossom, calling her "Dirty-Piglet-Stay-at-Home."

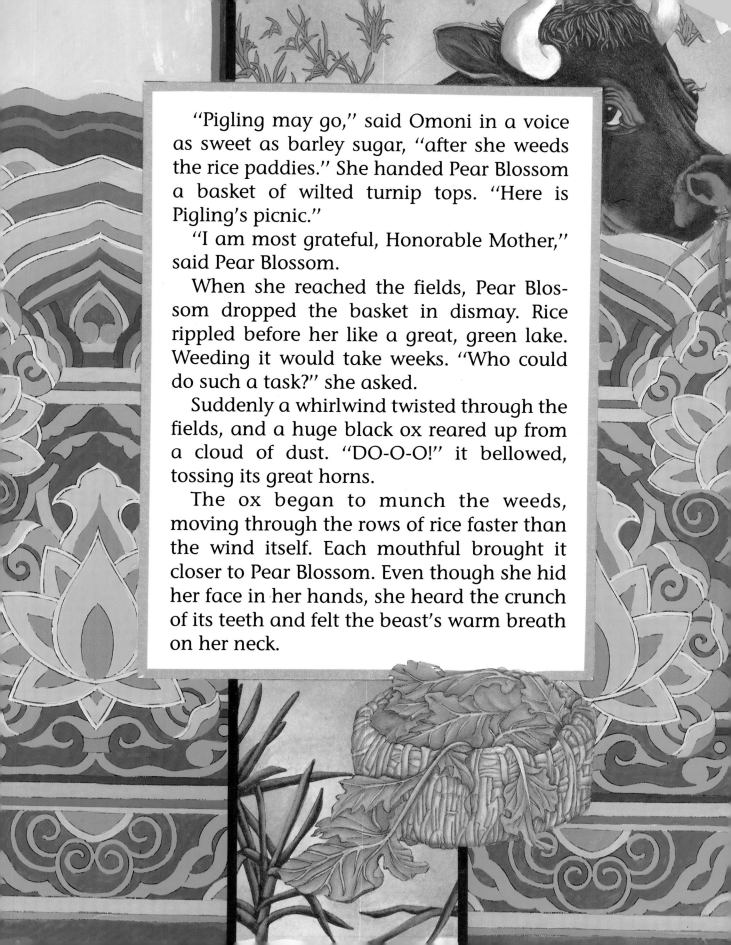

"Pigling may go," said Omoni in a voice as sweet as barley sugar, "after she weeds the rice paddies." She handed Pear Blossom a basket of wilted turnip tops. "Here is Pigling's picnic."

"I am most grateful, Honorable Mother," said Pear Blossom.

When she reached the fields, Pear Blossom dropped the basket in dismay. Rice rippled before her like a great, green lake. Weeding it would take weeks. "Who could do such a task?" she asked.

Suddenly a whirlwind twisted through the fields, and a huge black ox reared up from a cloud of dust. "DO-O-O!" it bellowed, tossing its great horns.

The ox began to munch the weeds, moving through the rows of rice faster than the wind itself. Each mouthful brought it closer to Pear Blossom. Even though she hid her face in her hands, she heard the crunch of its teeth and felt the beast's warm breath on her neck.

At last she dared to peek between her fingers. Both ox and weeds were gone. Hoofprints big as cartwheels pocked the field, yet not a single blade of rice was trampled. And when Pear Blossom looked in her basket, she found fruit and honey candy instead of turnips!

She bowed, then cupped her hands and called, "A thousand thanks!"

Pear Blossom hastened to the village festival. The road, which followed a crooked stream, was rough with pebbles. Pear Blossom had just slipped off one straw sandal to shake out a stone when she heard a shout.

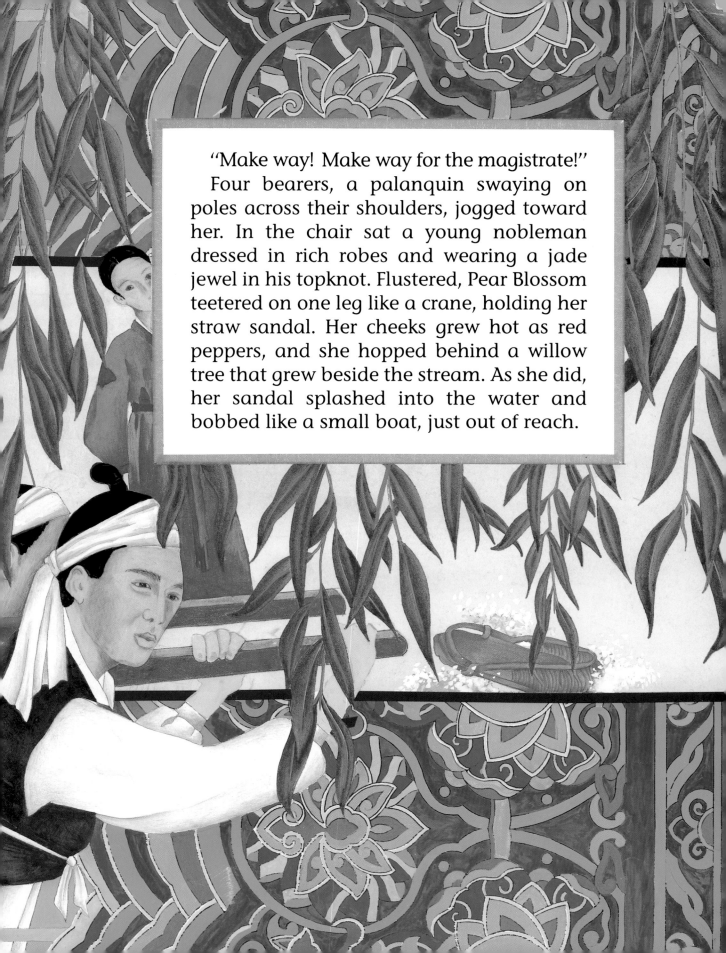

"Make way! Make way for the magistrate!"
Four bearers, a palanquin swaying on poles across their shoulders, jogged toward her. In the chair sat a young nobleman dressed in rich robes and wearing a jade jewel in his topknot. Flustered, Pear Blossom teetered on one leg like a crane, holding her straw sandal. Her cheeks grew hot as red peppers, and she hopped behind a willow tree that grew beside the stream. As she did, her sandal splashed into the water and bobbed like a small boat, just out of reach.

"Stop!" commanded the magistrate from his palanquin.

He was calling to his bearers. But Pear Blossom thought he was shouting at her, and, frightened, she fled down the road.

The magistrate gazed after Pear Blossom, struck by her beauty. Then he ordered his men to fish her sandal from the stream and to carry him back to the village.

At the festival Pear Blossom forgot about her missing shoe. She watched the acrobats and tightrope walkers until she was dizzy. She listened to the flutes and drums until her ears rang. She nibbled on treats until her basket was almost empty.

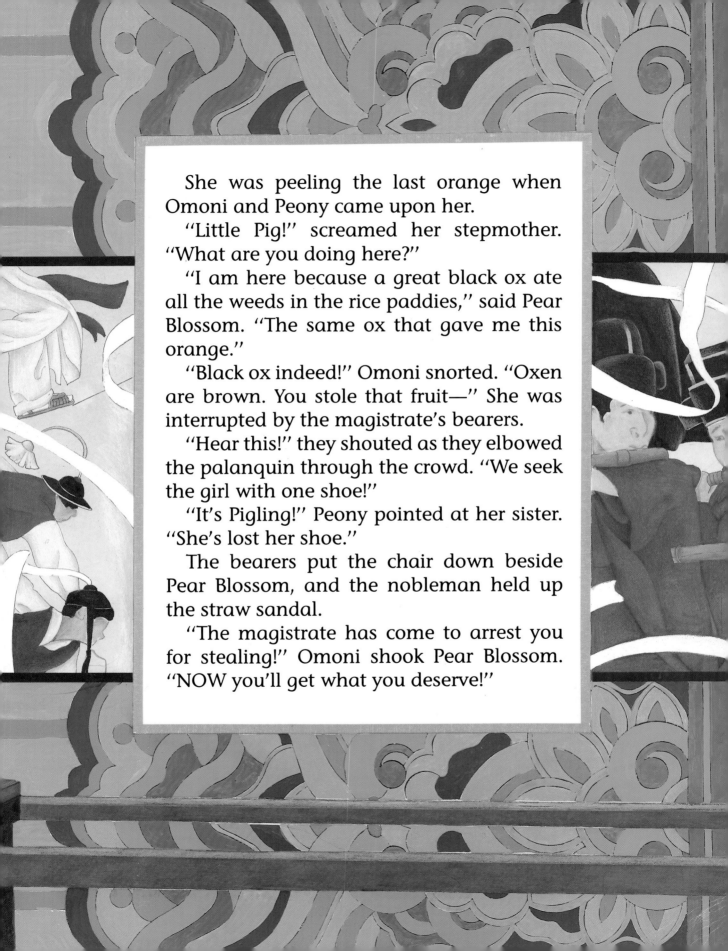

She was peeling the last orange when Omoni and Peony came upon her.

"Little Pig!" screamed her stepmother. "What are you doing here?"

"I am here because a great black ox ate all the weeds in the rice paddies," said Pear Blossom. "The same ox that gave me this orange."

"Black ox indeed!" Omoni snorted. "Oxen are brown. You stole that fruit—" She was interrupted by the magistrate's bearers.

"Hear this!" they shouted as they elbowed the palanquin through the crowd. "We seek the girl with one shoe!"

"It's Pigling!" Peony pointed at her sister. "She's lost her shoe."

The bearers put the chair down beside Pear Blossom, and the nobleman held up the straw sandal.

"The magistrate has come to arrest you for stealing!" Omoni shook Pear Blossom. "NOW you'll get what you deserve!"

"Then she must deserve *me* as her husband," said the magistrate, "for this lucky shoe has led me to her."

"Another of Pigling's magic tricks!" hissed Omoni, pulling Peony to the palanquin. "*My* daughter will give you TWO shoes! That is twice as lucky!"

The magistrate looked at Omoni as if she had lost her wits; then he turned to Pear

Blossom and said, "I've luck enough if she who wears *this* one becomes my bride."

Pear Blossom smiled, too shy to speak, and slipped the sandal on her foot.

Omoni stood staring, stiff as a clay statue, but Peony ran straight to the rice fields to find the magic ox. All she saw was a glimpse of its hooves as it galloped away.

When springtime came, the magistrate sent a go-between to Pear Blossom's old father to arrange a grand marriage. Pear Blossom's wedding slippers were of silk, and in the courtyard of her splendid new house, a dozen pear trees bloomed. "Ewha! Ewha!" chirruped the sparrows in the branches. "E-WHA!" croaked the giant frog down below.

That is as it was long ago, and as it should be. For, in Korea, *Ewha* means "Pear Blossom."

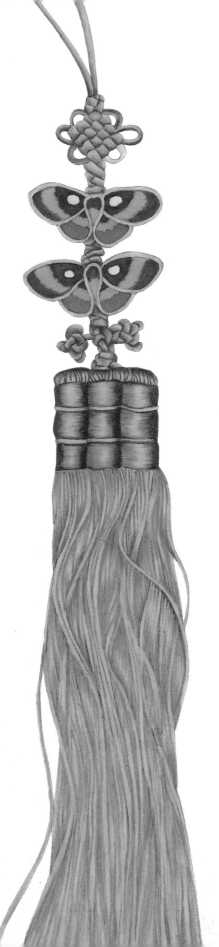

Author's Note

Many hundreds of Cinderella stories are told around the world. In Korea there are half a dozen versions. Although Pear Blossom is not always her name, the heroine is always a dutiful daughter and in the end prevails over her unkind stepmother and stepsister—or sisters. Most often she is rescued from her miserable life by an honorable official, although not necessarily by means of a shoe. In one version she escapes by dying and climbing to heaven on a rope.

Tokgabis, sometimes spelled *doggabbis*, often appear in Korean fairy tales. Sometimes kind-hearted, other times fearsome, these goblins help or trouble humans as they choose. Some people believe that they are the spirits of good people who have died. In this story the timely assistance of the frog, the sparrows, and the black ox are the work of a *tokgabi*, perhaps the spirit of Pear Blossom's own mother.

This retelling is based on three variations of a tale that has been a favorite of Korean children for centuries.

Illustrator's Note

The designs found on the cover and throughout this book were inspired by patterns painted on the eaves of Korean temples. These patterns are called "Tanchǒng." They are symbols of good luck, protection, and the cycle of reincarnation.

The pendants seen here and on the title page are worn as decoration on the "hanbok," the traditional women's dress that consists of two pieces—a skirt tied high under the arms by long ribbons and a short jacket. No buttons or hooks are used on either male or female dress.

The horsehair hat donned by Pear Blossom's father is the mark of a Korean gentleman.

The wedding ducks on page 42 are called "kirogi," and are a symbol of fidelity.

The long white ribbons seen in the festival illustrations are attached to the hats of men performing the traditional Farmers' Dance. As the men dance and toss their heads, the ribbons form graceful flowing patterns.

The information for these illustrations was gathered in Korea at museums and palaces, at festivals and concerts, and at a village set up to replicate the way Korean people lived three hundred years ago.

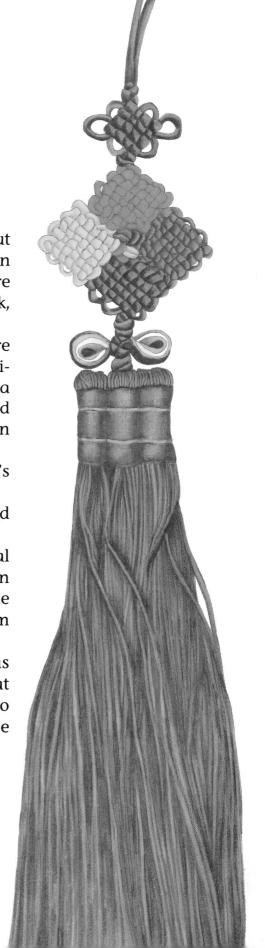